To Lil, Sky and Son for putting up with my occasional grumpy feet,
and to everyone who woke up with grumpy feet this morning,
I hope you find your baby unicorn.
L.S.

First published in Great Britain in 2016
by Boxer® Books Limited.
www.boxerbooks.com
Boxer® is a registered trademark of Boxer Books Limited.

Text and illustrations copyright © 2016 Lisa Stubbs

The illustrations were screen printed by the author.
The text is set in Goudy Old Style.

ISBN 9781910126769

1 3 5 7 9 10 8 6 4 2

Printed in China

Lily and Bear
Grumpy Feet

Lisa Stubbs

Boxer Books

Lily loved to draw,
but today something
felt different.

Things felt a little frumpy
and bumpy, just not so and
not quite right.

The day was
too rainy,

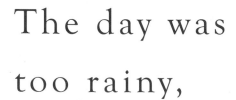

the teapot was
too dribbly
and the sunshine
colour was missing.

Lily's pencils were too pointy, her paint too sloshy and her crayons too stubby.

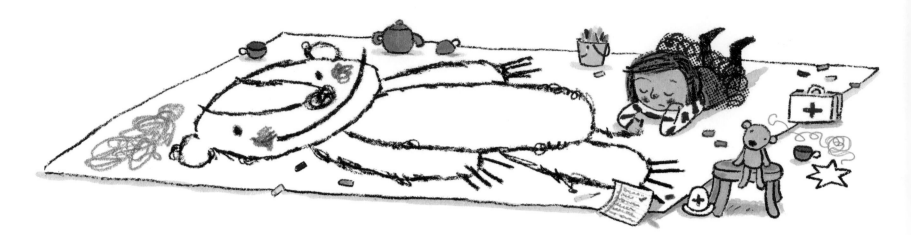

Everything felt grouchy and mouchy,
out of sorts and discombobbled.

Things to do... ✓
1. Draw bear
2. Drive to the moon
3. ~~fly~~ drink hot chocolate
4. polish stars
5. Jump really very high
6. find a baby unicorn

Until she drew . . .

Bear!

Bear put on his doctor's hat
and stethoscope and listened . . .

It was clear to Bear what was wrong . . .

Lily had

grumpy feet!

Bear thought it would help
if Lily wore happy shoes . . .

But things still felt frumpy and bumpy, just not so and not quite right.

Lily's feet were still grumpy.

Bear thought
it might help
if Lily had some
sticky cake.

But Lily's feet were
still grumpy.

Lily took her grumpy feet
to sit in the toy box.

Bear looked at Lily's list and
had a marvellous idea.

He set to work immediately . . .

Bear squeezed into the
toy box next to Lily
and started the engine.
"Where are we going?"
asked Lily.

Bear drove past the
rainy day, dribbly
teapot and missing
sunshine colour.
Past the pointy pencils,
sloshy paint and
stubby crayons.
Past the happy shoes
and sticky fishy cake.

"To a place that glows all comfy, not frumpy and bumpy. It is very so and just right," said Bear, as they drove into the starry night.

They drank hot chocolate and polished the stars. Then Bear played a happy moon tune on his banjo.

Lily's feet started to tap and smile.

Lily's feet started to wiggle and giggle.

Lily's feet started to laugh and jump . . . really very high!

Bear had turned the grumps
into the jumps!
There was only one thing left to do.

Number 6 on Lily's list.

Find a baby unicorn . . .

And they did.